MENU
fish
potatoes
tomatoes
fried eggs
pizzas
pineapples
cakes
pies
puddings
melons

For Anna

Fun-to-Read Picture Books have been
grouped into three approximate readability
levels by Bernice and Cliff Moon. Yellow
books are suitable for beginners; red books
for readers acquiring first fluency; blue
books for more advanced readers.

This book has been assessed as Stage 5
according to *Individualised Reading*, by
Bernice and Cliff Moon, published by
The Centre for the Teaching of Reading,
University of Reading
School of Education.

First published 1986 by
Walker Books Ltd
184-192 Drummond Street
London NW1 3HP

© 1986 Phyllis King

First printed 1986
Printed and bound by
L.E.G.O., Vicenza, Italy

British Library Cataloguing in Publication Data
King, Phyllis
The hungry cat.—(Fun-to-read picture books)
I. Title   II. Series
823'.914[J]   PZ7

ISBN 0-7445-0481-3

THE HUNGRY CAT

Written and
illustrated by
Phyllis King

WALKER BOOKS

LONDON

The hungry cat ate 1 fish.

The hungry cat ate 2 potatoes.

The hungry cat ate **3** tomatoes.

The hungry cat ate **4** fried eggs.

The hungry cat ate 5 pizzas.

The hungry cat ate **6** pineapples.

The hungry cat ate 7 cakes.

The hungry cat ate 8 pies.

The hungry cat ate **9** puddings.

The hungry cat ate 10 melons.

The hungry

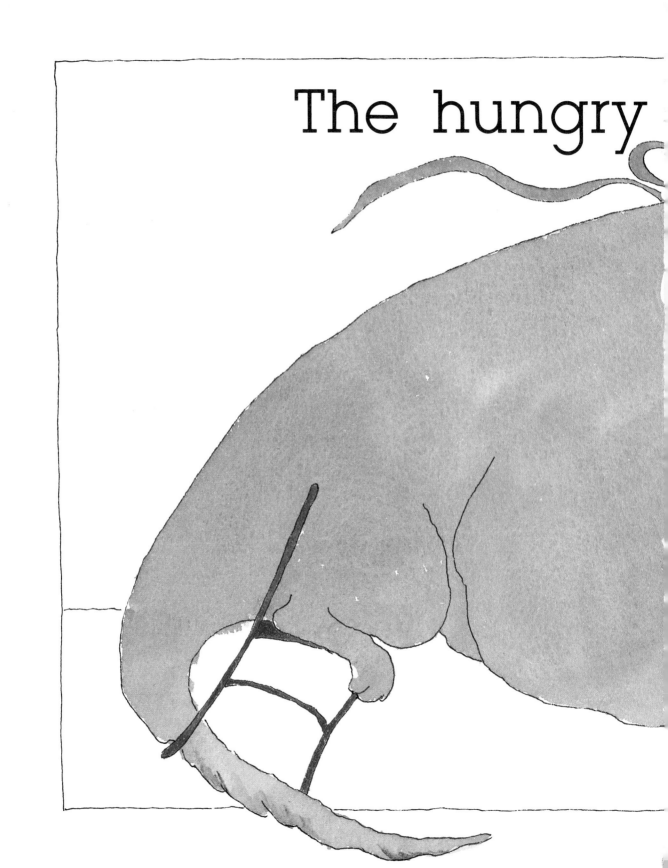

cat felt sick.

Up came the 10 melons.

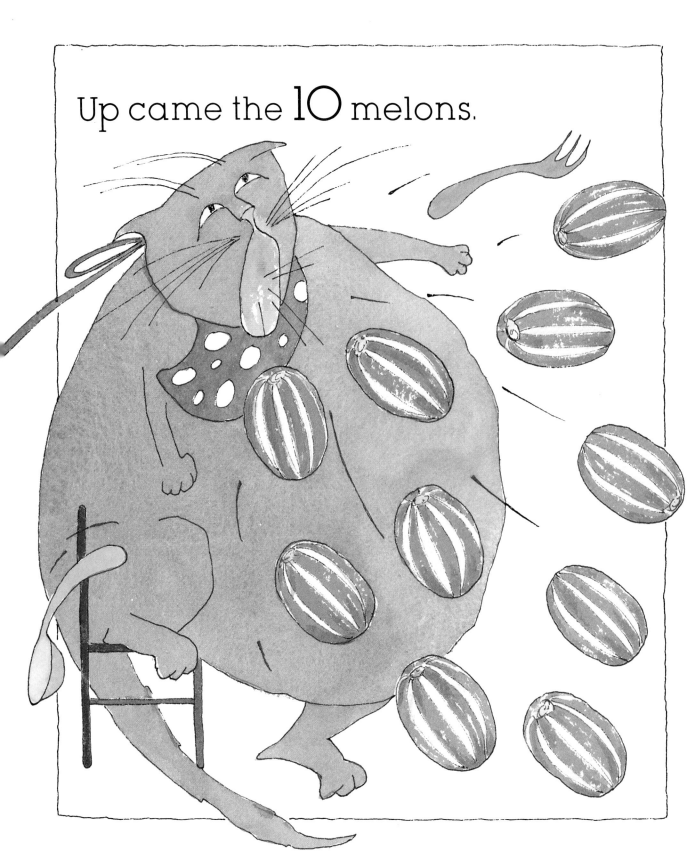

Up came the 9 puddings.

Up came the 8 pies.

Up came the 7 cakes.

Up came the **6** pineapples.

Up came the 5 pizzas.

Up came the 4 fried eggs.

Up came the **3** tomatoes.

Up came the 2 potatoes.

Up came the 1 fish.

'Now I feel hungry again,'
said the cat.